About the Author

David Vaughn wanted to be a writer when he was young. He read comics and was a huge horror buff. He still loves to do the things he does.

Strange Notions – Volume 1

David Vaughn

Strange Notions – Volume 1

Olympia Publishers
London

www.olympiapublishers.com
OLYMPIA PAPERBACK EDITION

Copyright © David Vaughn 2024

The right of David Vaughn to be identified as author of
this work has been asserted in accordance with sections 77 and 78 of
the Copyright, Designs and Patents Act 1988.

All Rights Reserved

No reproduction, copy or transmission of this publication
may be made without written permission.
No paragraph of this publication may be reproduced,
copied or transmitted save with the written permission of the publisher,
or in accordance with the provisions
of the Copyright Act 1956 (as amended).

Any person who commits any unauthorised act in relation to
this publication may be liable to criminal
prosecution and civil claims for damage.

A CIP catalogue record for this title is
available from the British Library.

ISBN: 978-1-83543-173-3

This is a work of fiction.
Names, characters, places and incidents originate from the writer's
imagination. Any resemblance to actual persons, living or dead, is
purely coincidental.

First Published in 2024

Olympia Publishers
Tallis House
2 Tallis Street
London
EC4Y 0AB

Printed in Great Britain

Dedication

To my cousin, Dominic Dontez Howard; my family; my future kids; and my people. I did this for us. (Myself.)

For the many and complex.

So-UL Caliber

The devil is a lie, and some of the most honest things about the interactions and discussions with the sort may be your fate being sealed. The situation this character finds himself in may depict that, and yes, it may be satirical.

If you ever heard of the man who sold his soul to play music, it would not be difficult to imagine the concept. For any person, to aspire to be something at the cost of their own life, eternal or not, is worthwhile, isn't it? They ask, "Is it delusional to be great?" Great, like a legend, or great like Billy the Kid. They say, "How delusional is it to be idolized and feared?"

To be remembered for anything with your name being cemented in the minds of those who knew the tales. So, that is how the story should be. How great a shot it was, or they hadn't seen shooting like that since one of those westerns! That is what this legend would be, and the cost was a good one—a fair trade in some respects. Say for something you can't see or touch like a soul. In exchange for an object that will become whatever I need to make a legend.

Looking at it at first, the weird smell and even the faint whispers did not distract any thoughts. The glint, even through the rust, was amazing, and all it cost was a piece of paper. That's it—not even with a name on it. They said he would remember they met. Funny, because the name and face vanish from the mind. He really cannot say how the conversation started. The legend for this generation is "what will be remembered." Count on that s%&$.

The deaths were not planned, nor was their escape, but how good it is when these types don't get caught. What kind of legend goes that quick? They count and don't say whether it is one of a dozen deaths. Only a few may go down with this kind of legacy, and they say they have "deadly aim"—not too many misses. Managed to kill one of them with a warning shot. Legend, running will never make the paper for those types. The legend will say, not since the O.K. Corral have they seen shootings like this!

The mass murderer, *huh?* They say the killings won't stop. We all may see that is a legend they're speaking of, and we should correct it as soon as possible. They'll say that they may have even killed a person over a drink, and who would for not speaking correctly. The years and deaths add up.

It's getting harder to see the hows and whats of it, and they say for sure that this killer may have been shot more than a dozen times. What we know is that the legend can't only be a murderer. It's getting harder to see, that's all. The legend will say that with an aim like that, they could not see. They got to be able to see, though, because they won't miss. Tears for fears, I guess.

Fade in and out with trembling hands and shallow breathing… A murderer, naw, we know that the real story is that we've all been speaking of a legend. Deaths included, now they just wished it would stop.

Zycadelic

A bunch of nervous thoughts that I had never thought about before. With every minute and second feeling like I would either piss on myself or that my thoughts would come pouring out of my head and run around the small two-bedroom apartment.

Thoughts about the what-could-be scenarios. Covered with the idea of traveling and standing still all in one moment. "Yes," it had been a while since I felt that nervous. Even my sweat would have sweat, but the idea of sweat even bothered me only because it was not distracting enough.

With the strange sounds emanating from the other room serving as reason enough to be distracted, I looked in to see. Not shocked by the sound now that I could see where it had come from. I was more interested in who it was that stared at the screen. With a flash, it turned off. Not staring at me, my roommate got up and switched the TV back on. Startled by his quick motions, I spoke.

After a few brief words about the upcoming pizza delivery, I began to forget about what made me nervous in the first place. His startling reaction to my presence was not startling.

To myself, I think about what I am thinking about. I think again to myself about how it is not his personality I am noticing, but it was his unsettling reaction to "something." I mistakenly asked, "Yo," as if the word was a cue for him to depart. He definitely shot me a quick glance and left. Startled were my initial thoughts on his reaction, which I will one day recognize as fear.

Over the next few days, we came and went, and what I felt nervous about had soon left my mind. The weather was not much of a distraction, but I guess, by chance, I spent more time away from home. On the few occasions when we were home together, our conversations never touched base on what he was watching that day. Even now, the only thing that makes me bring it up is that I saw him watching it again just recently. I didn't see much of it and heard what I thought was a muffled voice. One that almost made me laugh but seemed to frighten him some, which caused him to tense his jaw. The colors, though.

I didn't see my roommate that day or that evening, but in his room, I could hear the television working. You know what it is like when somebody plays a game, and it sounds so interesting you want to join. This was one of those times I got up to go and ask him to let me play, but before I could get to his door, there he was. I noticed the TV was off because the sound was no longer playing. I asked him then what was up, but not in a threatening way, and he said nothing and made some joke about alone time.

"Relief," but it is like I said—the sounds were funny, so maybe he has some online girl or "something." The following weeks were the same: rent came and went. Here we were again with the delivery day for pizza night, and he asked me, "Yo, check this out."

Now, my roommate and I are buddies and had been for some time. We kept very little from one another. So, at the thought of his prompt, I was ready to see what he was talking about. He took me to the living room and stood, looking from me to the television and said nothing. I stared at the blank screen and "waited." Nothing. And so it went—nothing from him and not much change on the screen, but I noticed that he became more relaxed. We watched some weird shows a couple of times, but nothing sexual. "Cool."

It never made sense why he moved out. I called the number he left to get in contact with him a few times, but not much came from the calls other than distracted conversations and weird background sounds. He even answered in a fearful voice once or twice. One night, my phone rang at some odd hour and stopped too quickly for me to answer. I suppose it was him, but who knows.

I guess to somebody it makes sense. But for my "roommate," it may never make sense why those soundful colors moved that way, and it never will.

Clocks

"Excellently," said Darby. A brief pause of laughter with a joke still lingering in the air, alongside the smoke from the incense lighting his nostrils. The laughter was more satisfying than he could have explained. Still packing with fervent motions and less time than outside activities should have allowed for such crude behavior. The time ticked away.

Still trying to hide the giddy behavior as the car was filled with odds and ends that would make the trip, the stay, and the return easier to manage. He overlooked the large package that sat in the back seat. Overlooked as in looked to make sure it was securely fastened. Hmph of satisfaction. "Still more time passed."

Answering the phone while driving made him somewhat distracted from the conversation. Not thinking about how far off his memory would drift. Or if the questions would take his mind into some distant dimension.

The wheres and the whos of it being a portal that he would only return from after he arrived at the cabin. So, the question was answered as he shut the door. "Yes, he would do it, and thanks for giving him a call," he said as he hung up. "New companion."

Opening the door for himself and the odds and ends for the trip had begun to bring back the familiar sense that made the trip worthwhile. Yes, the feeling of nostalgia settling in and, yes, the sentimental sayings that may go along with these types of trips.

Sayings like "Good as Gold" or "Good for the Gander." "*Hmph,* yeah. Time has passed."

Unloading the car had been a breeze, and nobody complains when things are going well. The extra time gave him a way to go over what he may have said if it was to go how it should. Thinking it over, letting the warmth from the furnace settle into the room... Time passed.

"Remember, in dusk, we say..." Trying to think if he would leave it as dusk or dust before he was struck by a short bout of laughter. Laughter that was brought on by how overly emotional those words may have been. His or anybody's words, but then more seriously, he thought nobody really would laugh. Nine a.m. flashing over and over again. Sitting down to think over what or how he could explain it... "Time passed."

The trip went well as expected, backing out of the long road that led up to the cabin he and his off-and-on-again companions had shared. All packages were delivered, thinking about how his words would be as he spoke. It had been some time since anyone had seen him, and the time had passed. Yes, time had passed for them. That is, however, time passed for those off-and-on companions that he left buried there. Yes, sure, he would speak during the eulogy—they were his friends. And the search had been given up so so long ago that it was time for everyone to enter a time of mourning.

He thinks about what it sounded like as they whispered to him about needing him to come back and bring a buddy, and he did. He did come back to them, leaving the packages where he would leave them from time to time.

Yes, he thought as the whispers got louder. Already it was near time for another visit and so soon after he left. Giddy already with the idea, he answered his phone as it rang. Listening, he obediently turned toward his new companions, listening for the whispers. "Yes, and time will pass"—for those as well.

Mr. Sexy

The day breeze and golden rays playing upon his tresses. Much applause to his shape and cheerful demeanor. I watch. "So funny, Mr. Sexy, what beautiful shoes you have."

"Mr. Sexy, how wonderful it is to hear you speak again."

Do they enjoy the conversation? Is that genuine laughter playing across their faces? I wonder.

Madness drifts across the places of flesh and people... "What is this? Is this a storm brewing, Mr. Sexy?

How could this be? I am sure I paid it on time." "I beg to differ," is the imagined response. A response that seems as automatic as the ATM teller that he stares at frustratingly.

"I hope you enjoyed my letters, Mr. Sexy. I do so hope you did...

"Hello again, Mr. Sexy. I noticed your kitchen light was on, so I turned it off for you. Mr. Sexy, don't worry; nobody will see. Your house needs cleaning. We won't disappoint.

"Not feeling well, Mr. Sexy? Those are only laxatives, Mr. Sexy. Why don't you take one of those antacids you've been talking about? Don't worry, they help with digestion.

"My letters amuse me, don't they? And we have gotten so used to your messes, but don't worry, we will fix them... *tsk, tsk.*

"Look, don't worry. It was a natural reaction. We can't have you making those same choices, Mr. Sexy, can we? We just need to adjust ourselves, don't we?

"A slip, a fall, and, oops, but you sure are sturdy, Mr.

Sexy..."

Of course, you signed it that way, but still, you couldn't be what I thought. Oops, but how could it be that easy to use my name? "Never mind, you say."

"We all make mistakes, Mr. Sexy, and we will be more careful next time, won't we?

"Mr. Sexy, how happy you seem as we watch ourselves, don't we? Never mad, are they, us and me. We cannot be there here tonight, can we? Don't worry, they won't see us—them. Mr. Sexy."

Bite

With better things on my mind than the mundane activities that surround me, my own livelihood and enjoyment are more important than, say, these people. The morose skin color and translucent personalities only add to the fervent anger of my emotions. As they dwell with ever-frustratingly dull footsteps around me, I can count the regular and ordinary thoughts on their minds.

"What's this?" A look of disdain by some person has passed by my scowled features, and none too suddenly has the look passed has this "figure" escaped. "*Hmph*." I let a short chuckle pass my lips, and this is done with the joy that I have shocked their meager existence—those that have surrounded me with such distasteful appearances. No pizzazz, no true flare. Wow, what nothingness. The face, though, this person had the nerve to pass me by with. That face and not without much else. It lingers.

The lingering is not without effect, whoever you were. This is true, and, yes, with jealous intent and harm in mind, I followed you. "Yes." I watched as you were alone and almost thought you may have noticed me stifling my laughter as I saw that same look you used on another's face. "Petty, yes," but not impatient. Whoever that was, I almost envy the fact that this "person" could share that look with one such as you. I passed by you on the sidewalk, and all it took was a look in another direction. "Pity," I thought that you may have been deeper. Was I wrong to have chosen you? Could my patience be wrong? Was it mere coincidence? But then, what about "any" others that may have shared that likeness? That look to stare and not recognize me? To see me and not understand them with such weak pallor. No, I believe that "YOU" are different.

I decide to find out if this is fate playing a rare game on me, so I leave a letter. "Yes, of course, it was blank." I will let you describe what it says. I watched as you looked around with a bit of annoyance on your face. My mind is made up. We will meet.

The sunlight fades into the dusk. You and I have come to know so well. Sorry that our acquaintance may not be as pleasing to us both. I have watched you for a year now, painstakingly aware of "Alone you are." My mind has slipped into what I feel is best suited for this meeting. Now my anger and jealousy have been stirred. That face, I must see you make it again.

Forgetful you.

The idea that you could have been deeper is revealed as your blood-curdling screams can be heard through the neighborhood. "*Hmph.*"

I Got an Itch

The itching and burning under my skin are irritating. What may be more irritating is my stuffy nose. I mean, when is it ever fun to have a stuffy nose? I can guess and say never.

I cannot wait to scratch my armpit is all I can think. I even have an apparatus for those hard-to-reach places. I hope that I do not have any more accidents like before.

The burning… My skin just will not cool down, and just like a dummy, I went and had another accident. I even had to change underwear because of it. Now, I'm going to be late for work.

I like to drive my car. I liked it even more without my stuffy nose. I am going to blame my neighbor's pets for this. I do not want to be dismissed from work because of a little cold. My throat hurts.

People make me so angry sometimes. Complain and itch, some guy I thought I knew complains to me about how I should be near him and that I look sick. His angry stares don't scare me, though. I take a long stare at him through the bottom of my water cup from the cooler.

The complaints and the itching won't stop me now. I cannot wait for the lunch and dinner meetings. It's when all the executives plan and talk about stuff. I cannot think about what the meeting is called. I do not like what's his name.

My head hurts, but it is a funny feeling. I've never fallen asleep at work before, but, hey, there is a first time for everything. They wanted to call a doctor, but I said, "Hey, it's cool, man." I can make it home just fine. I think people are happy for me, but I can see a lot of angry faces. "That's some nice sweat you got working over there," they say. I don't like their angry comments.

My sweat burns the scratches all over my skin, and at home, I cannot wait to see. Part in shock and another in fear. I look at the deep lacerations I must have gotten in my raw skin. It burns...

I'm so pumped to see people tomorrow, so I can see the way they think. My thoughts seem funny, and now I like what they think. I will see them there. My fuzzy mind does not mind getting up off the bathroom floor. My sleep must have come for me early. No matter, I can hear it taste their thoughts, and I cannot be late...

Love Lives... I Guess

I can't imagine a day without it. Without her, the way she smelled or the type of perfume that even her friends used. I said that because I knew that she would not be far from them, at least sometimes. I had crushes back then...

I could not imagine not being able to see her smile. Or at times imagining that I would be somebody that she would laugh for. Thinking to myself how lucky I was that my attention and hers would connect. She was special then...

Later, at some point, I would remember when we would exchange letters. I would remember that it was not just how she looked, but the way she made me feel. I would think that despite outside noises, her voice or mine would rise above most of it. Maybe I would remember it that way...

I think about not always being there and laugh to myself sometimes about something she may have said. At times, they would hear them, too.

I think about liking the way her clothes fit.

I wanted to admire her daily, and I did often, but it still did not seem like enough. I wasn't greedy, and I do not think she was, but the feeling seemed both satisfying and insatiable at times.

Dissatisfied Thoughts

Her hunger would show. She waved at me, and I would wave back; the motion rehearsed in my mind over and over again until it was a hug she gave me—satisfying and maddening.

Mentally collapsing the first time I did not see her, my days were incomplete without her. My emotions were empty and lost without directions.

The first series of questions about whereabouts seemed routine.

I never saw her again, at least not in that way or form. Heartbroken and lost without her. Many pieces of her and the way she made me feel lost, at least to some.

She was never found, not all of her anyway—a piece of clothing here or there, strange letters hidden around her last known whereabouts and home. Pictures that they hadn't known she'd take...

That is what it is like when "stalkers" take an interest in someone. And like I said, I never saw her again, and time had passed. Which it always does...

So, I forgot partly—I mean not wholly and completely, but for my own best interest, as my therapist suggests. You know what else? Even I could figure out that her letters were real...

When did I receive them or why couldn't they see them or crazy suggestions like why don't I read them to them? Like I would do that...

I did, however, begin to tell stories about the letters, only because I was prompted to. The stories depicting how my love would be returned or how when I would receive the letters, she was glad she sent them. Love lived and so did I.

The therapist would one day suggest that I should give up on the silly notion that these love letters were real. The realness of those letters even had me under investigation—an investigation that eventually led to a short and horrific stay in a mental facility. Even then, the letters did not stop, and sure enough, they took them, even though, they were addressed to me. Very rude. The rudeness, however, had to be excused because A) they were addressed to me from her B) security purposes C) due to A and B, they proved that I had not gone mad.

So, the investigations continued…

"What did the letters say?" they would ask, and I would only gauff at them in response, clearly baffled that they could not see the beautiful handwritten letters, just empty pages. Not noticing the perfect manuscript letter and curves of her words showing how she had grown. It had been years, and she mentioned how strong she had gotten. I laughed, loving the notion. She was ready to meet, but first, there would be things I would have to do first. She would send the instructions, and I would obey.

First, she needed to see who began my sessions. Not the therapist, but who really thought that I would need that and not her. It would take some time, but I would find them. When I did, I realized it was my neighbor who noticed me skulking about. I thought that, yes, maybe she could help them understand. She said she could…

I remember the evening that their photos appeared on the news, and worried faces all about saying they couldn't understand, or what a sweet couple, and they never could have imagined. Nobody ever really expects the worst, but sometimes those things happen. Things like disappearances, which should be normal to people here, but, "hey," I guess it is not like it was their love or anything but "hey." In her next few letters, she said she would explain, and she did...

She told me she needed to make space for the times that she may call. She called me once, and people did not see that it wasn't a prank call and wouldn't give me the phone. She explained that my neighbors may have known that she was interested in hooking up and may have conspired to stop her late-night calls and visits. Typical, but like I said, she would explain it to them, and never mind the pieces of clothes that belonged to her in my neighbor's junk box. I figured this would be similar. I mean, why would anyone care about that? It is not like it was their favorite shirt to see her wear or anything. So again, "we," or me and "her," would need to see who else listened to our conversations.

She explained that she needed me to speak with an old friend of mine who looked at her funny once when she told somebody I was cute. I could find him and bring him to her so she and I could confront him. She had agreed and told me not to watch, and I promised that I wouldn't. When I contacted him, he made fun of me at first because it had been years since we had spoken. I let my anger pass and did not let him in on our secret. He agreed to meet, so I considered "us"—him and I—even.

I wouldn't forget the sound he made, like a gasp. What is that, shock? *Hmm,* not one for the gym, because he did not seem to be in shape for whatever she discussed with him. The whole time whimpering about how he made a mistake and couldn't bear the thought of it. Even saying he did not see her... All through guttural screams, I can't explain; she could. She explained that he was supposed to send me a message to meet her somewhere, and he must not have thought it was a good idea because he didn't. Sometime later, she disappeared, so it must have skipped his mind.

Pfft, some friend...

Lastly, before she was really ready to see me again, she wanted me to prove I really loved her. I asked how, and she told me she would explain. I couldn't wait...

I knew that what she explained was best. How nobody understood how we felt about one another or how no one really knew her. She told me she understood how I felt and that the two of us could not exist without each other. So, when she said she would come for me, I understood that she was right.

I knew that to exist without her wouldn't be right, and I jokingly thought about how I had lived wrong for far too long. She would laugh at what I said and had told me before that she hadn't laughed much since they made her leave. I felt she was accurate, noting that she had mentioned that "they" made her leave. We had no secrets from one another before and definitely not now. I knew that she would have told me if it was important.

To believe in her was all it took for me to prove I loved her, and I proved that by going to where she would meet me. I got the message from the person who posed as my friend. "They" were jealous of us, is what I believed, and I did not try to explain because I knew that she would know the truth. She came for me that night...

Her embrace made me scream at first. Her bite felt as long as life had been without her. Her touch warmed as she held me. Held me so tight that I dared not scream. My breath would become hers, and I gladly and longingly gave it to her. I felt ecstasy from my pain, feeling my emotions become like hers. I faded away blissfully that night, and I knew that I would exist inside her and between her and around her, feeling eternally in her embrace. Love lives... I guess.

They Made Me Do It

The forms of possession are as follows: ownership—I saw it first, and it is mine—finders keepers, and finally, satanic or demonic. There may be more forms of possession, but we will leave that for later discussion.

Coordinating between activities takes more deliberate action than his current mood would tolerate, at least for long periods of time. The seconds between noticing the screen go into a pause phase when random pictures appear and the thoughts passing across his mind had not distracted from the annoying buzz of the useless fan.

The hum did not really create a cool thinking environment, but an environment that was filled with stale air and wrong answers. Deciding to let the screen enter into a phase again took almost as much deliberation in answering the work on the screen. Sitting and resisting the urge to get up and play the game, finally, as the screen entered the pause phase and as pictures floated into vision, it was clear that the assignment could wait. Released from the tension of having attempted the work and even more relaxed with the thought that the work would become easier if he studied, he kicked himself for attempting to do the assignment without studying but proud that the answers would be in sight…

Fevered Dreams and Irrational Thoughts

His next attempt at doing the work came much easier after he had time to read over the actual instructions, which made his previous brazen attempt at doing the work laughable even to himself. How could he know to carry the two or plug in for any composite with a prime number? It made even more sense once the directions had been read. He enjoyed the work, and it relaxed his mind. He enjoyed the work even more once he figured out the puzzle or riddle based on the answers given. "Oh," I suppose that had not been explained. The point of the assignment was to crack a code and solve a riddle. A very exciting assignment.

"Deluded actions with nervous movement, excited eyes, and weary thoughts. No, prayers won't find these."

Signing his name across the paper would seal the deal. He knew what he had accomplished: he solved the puzzle, and the work would be delivered. The family that he slaughtered wouldn't mind the feat. I mean, they were there for the entire thing, singing in screams or what he perceived as bad "satanic mutterings." The Father's name signed across the envelope in somewhat similar fashion by him as he obeyed his spirit and became "like" him, a family man who enjoyed games and puzzles.

He had been there for almost nine days, the perfect amount of time. Not long enough for the entryways too close and too short for them to feel he and the others stayed too long. "Perfect."

When or if he is ever caught, he will say, "The devil made me do it," but we all know the truth, however. It was his shared love of family, beliefs, and puzzles.

Another Time and Place

The sun had dried up most of the rain from the previous day, which left small brown puddles in the places where the water could pool. She imagined the pools being large enough to allow people to swim in them—well, at least her. With that thought, she let her mind fog in and out of lucid patterns that would dissipate with faint and muffled sounds. She wanted a cigarette; she knew that the pools would not allow her to swim to the bottom, and she knew that the sky would not open and pull her into the clouds. Both distant and childish thoughts did not satisfy her cravings. "Muffled gasp."

The sounds that would bring some reaction to her were largely ignored. She was, however, more distracted with the thoughts of how long it would take for a puddle to dry up. She wondered if she could sit and watch, believing that logically it could happen since it did not take days or months for the other puddles to dissipate. She pondered this as she imagined that maybe someone else had decided to take a trip to the bottom of the pool, thinking maybe they could take the time away from her. She let the anger drive her thoughts away from parting the clouds. Her anger became so great that she stood from where she had been sitting, staring at the puddle, and marched over to the nearest one. "Muffled gasp."

"Thick clouds of smoke escaping her lungs."

With smoke filling her lungs, she decided to get a closer look. Peering down into the deeper-than-usual pool, she could make out her features. Letting the smoke escape her lungs into her reflection, for a few brief seconds, she could almost notice a slight difference in the smoke-filled image. Leaning closer, she, maybe, could hear a voice. Leaning closer still, she could see the culprit swimming there somewhere deep into the puddle. "Snatch." Harshly pulled into the water headfirst, where the rest of her just did not fit. It was a wonder how anyone else could swim there because she couldn't. Held there for five minutes or maybe thrashed wildly. To many, it would seem as if she was a street performer doing some wild new dance. To others, she was overreacting, they thought, and to an even smaller few, they would swear they saw a pair of strong hands smash her face into the small pool. "To many of us, though, we know now that it really is finders keepers."

A Whole New Scene

Driving and getting tired does not bode well for a person who has to drive for a living. It is not that the job is overtly lucrative, as in a sense that it gives the additional bragging rights associated with hard work, but in this case, it is almost everything but hard work. Other than the occasional bad passenger, the side hustle pays a little bit more so that the office cubicle is not a form of constraint or shackles. Complete with cramped corners, lack of desk space, and associating funny odors with the other cramped employees. Yes, being a driver had its benefits, but this trip, for odd reasons, had taken a toll.

No, not that it was the passenger, which can at times be problematic for some when they either do not enjoy small talk or are preoccupied with driving. No, the passenger, strangely quiet, did not say much even when greeted. Almost staring blankly when asked if the location was the right one, the passenger just stared and immediately departed when the location was reached. Fine, remember to tip or rate the trip is what should have been mentioned. But really, who forgets to rate the trip? Almost no one.

Those thoughts and others would pass back and forth in a rattled skull that had just banged itself against a harder-than-expected steering wheel. Harder still if it begins to steal away consciousness, bright lights approaching with a blaring sound means that people are going to be rescued to some...

It's hard to clear the mind when the mind is not sure why it is in such a fuss. The mind may have an even harder time finding itself when it cannot remember the last time it had seen a clock. Seeing people pulled from the car sent off cheers for others, but apparently not many were there to witness this heroic feat. The patient's explanation of how this was a terrible accident and that we were all lucky that no one was seriously injured was funny because it was unclear how bad the memory could become. Sleep maybe has a side effect, possibly and maybe, but possibly. Staring into the distance, letting the fading images of the now-burning car, and not seeing the at-first assumed ambulance, darkness comes.

    Awakened by a sharp pain and lack of motor skills as in hands and feet. Letting the shock sink in as the pale faces of once-known employees and one or two passengers came into view. Then, letting the sadness and fear sink in when the realization that this was a bonfire and that human meat was the main course. Letting out a sad groan as the knife slid into the belly and pulled out mostly sober and tired blood. Staring wide-eyed as the assumed EMS workers took turns licking the blade as they passed it around. Darkness did not come as quickly as some would hope. You know what some might have thought, 'The side hustle took its toll on him and killed 'em.' What many people could see by now, like these had shouted, "I saw it first, and it is mine!" Maybe a spleen, pancreas, some other small unknown organ…

Correspondence

I wanted to let the signals guide me. How could I feel so neglected after living such a self-indulgent life? A short list of itinerary: (1) Get up at seven a.m., stretch, yawn, eat a small breakfast. (2) Around eight a.m. to nine a.m., hop into my luxury sedan and drive the very lax fifteen minutes to work. (3) Nine thirty a.m. to ten a.m., walk into my highly over-the-top office on the bottom floor. (4) All of the things that I used to say kiss my ass.

As I prepare to tell another a**hole to pucker up, I could see the tension lines in their face. The small pockmarks on their skin did not look craterish but more like scarring from a bad burn. The acrid look of the clothes and his hair almost made me laugh. I did not; my high salary would not allow it, nor would my personality. I backed away from my desk to give a greeting to this person who had just entered my office. No words left his lips as he cleared his throat and looked me in the eye. Startled and not annoyed, I took the letter and opened it, not remembering when he handed it to me or how he left.

A message written directly to me and written in non-descript handwriting. Not cursive, but regular stationary words. I was surprised that the letter spoke of some of the things around me. Directions that described other directions, bored with the handwriting and not the game of cat and mouse. I wondered if it would make sense to call the police. My luxury sedan would easily take me to the nearest station. I ignored the notion. "No, I want to see what's behind the curtain." I followed the directions.

Letting my hands grip the wheel, I turned onto a familiar street. I had followed the letter's directions, only to end up in a place that I had seen many times before. Not one to linger, I felt that the senseless act of "following" would not have made me who I was. But I wanted to follow the signals, so I stayed.

My visit to this familiar street had not dulled my intentions. If anything, they only increased my want for "something." My lack of boredom and curiosity about the situation let my mind drift. Time passed, and I saw nothing. But with my short list of itineraries, it would be easy to keep "correspondence" to "follow," so I went home.

I watched as the familiar pockmarked face showed on the news. "Found dead at the scene" was how they put it. When asked if any witnesses saw anything, most said they saw nothing. With my mouth shut, I watched as a person described a "person" cruising the neighborhood in a luxury sedan. No one laughed…

My car was not shown, but I knew that the closeness of the subject matched too well. I wanted to follow the signals.

I began receiving phone calls shortly after "the news." I remember not paying attention to how long I had spoken with the anonymous caller. I remember the strange sense of nothingness; I remember being late to work and not remembering why. My short list of itinerary had become something else. "I was not a follower," not then…

My life never unraveled after the changes; it kind of just went as usual. The comings and goings of traffic, my on-and-off again itinerary—my life never really changed, so I continued to look for the signals.

The draft of air inside the room made the night cold but welcoming. The man or figure outside my home almost belonged. I could see that they wanted to know if I kept correspondence. Had I known that I would get the signal, my reason and I awaited "Correspondence."

"There was no sign of forced entry," they said. Police scouring, looking for clues to the grisly murder. The luxury sedan was still parked in the driveway. It had taken months to find the body, the only clues being the letters people thought were being answered. "A slaughter," they would call it, almost ritualistic. Looking for reasons as to how this could happen, all they could find was a short itinerary.

Later, no one noticed as the Sedan pulled into the yard…

She did not remember how long they had spoken, this man with the horrible scars.

She did not like the way he smelled. She did not know why she let them in.

She only wanted to read the messages…

I Got an Itch Too

Having the same nagging feeling of forgetfulness, not like forgetting what you are going to say but similar. Looking over at the other passengers of the crowded train station, the noise and distant smells do not arouse. What is interesting is the news coverage that sounded something like, "Breaking news: there has been an incident involving a man being bitten and being shot." How the two were connected was unclear, but the ridiculousness of the connection is how the stifling laughter almost caused the information about a possible outbreak of some sort to be missed.

As the train pulled in to let the passengers board, the smells slowly rolled away into concern and then shock. Looking over at the passengers, it was clear that one or two of them were battling the flu, with vomit included. The shock of not being able to see what this person had eaten recently and the shock of questioning what could produce anything similar to that color. Murmurs rose, and others were saying and asking, "Was that blood that this person is vomiting?" They still boarded the train, which annoyed no one, but the idea was the same for all other passengers: to give these persons a wide berth. As space was made in the already shrinking compartment, it was not difficult to see how poorly the health of some of the passengers was. As the train left the station and headed downtown, it made no quick assertion of one of the convulsing passengers.

Part of the way downtown (a short trip), one of the passengers who appeared to be asleep had been stirred awake.

With a distant look and foggier conversation, mumbles of hunger—fresh or maybe flesh—and the unmistakable word brain. This was not the convulsing passenger but yet another who had seemed to look sick and persistent. The convulsing passenger had already regained their composure, which could be a good part of that person's day beside the constant and horrible nosebleeds.

Pulling into the downtown station, which really had not responded to the health of the passengers, it could be heard loudly in the distance: directions on what to do if anyone had any of the following symptoms. The lengthy list mentioned much of what the passengers had experienced, minus the possible cough.

The amusement soon wore off as a crowd witnessed a stranger bite another. The shock and suddenness of the attack may be what frightened them, but many would say that it was the look of what may have been corpses rising in the station. How did anyone not see this…

Dark Fate: Photographs (Prolog)

Nothing could have happened without the first trip. And the second trip would only be the beginning of another bad story, but what if that could be different? What if...

Nothing could have happened without the second trip. The first trip would only be the beginning of another bad story, but what if that could be different? What if...

Letting the feeling of déjà vu rinse all over him, he listened to the recording, trying to find the place he left off. Not knowing how or why his attention had left the voices he had recorded, he found it odd to hear the sound of his own voice and wondered why he made such a recording. Taking into account the lost feeling of words he never said, words on the tip of the tongue but clear in the mind that the thoughts had been lost. It seemed as if those words were repeated, listening again and again for the muse that had those rephrased and repeated words.

"Crash." People arriving on the scene already knew that this would not be a lifesaving event. The helicopters that may have been used to save lives will now be used to overhead the traffic. The horrific crash was only witnessed by moviegoers in its sickening and devastating effects., with no survivors left. It was clear that finding the source of how this incident happened would require questioning the witnesses. Not that they would be imprisoned, but to find out how this happened. It will be remembered that anything that had been involved in such a crash did not survive.

Shocking himself awake to the screeching of the tires, he glanced to the left to see his buddy mindlessly not focusing on the road. A very uncharacteristic trait that suddenly appeared, one that he himself will be the source of many nightmares for himself and the driver of the very large semi. Again, listening to the ending of the tape about how things could be different and drifting off again. Faintly rubbing the side of his neck that in some distant universe may have been twisted and snapped into some odd angle. An angle that did not immediately take life but one that left him unable to move while he watched his friend bleed out all over the steering wheel from wounds that he could not see.

Nothing could have happened without the first trip. And the second trip would only be the beginning of another bad story, but what if that could be different? What if...

Nothing could have happened without the second trip. The first trip would only be the beginning of another bad story, but what if that could be different?

He had mindlessly recorded that odd voiceover and was becoming confused about whether or not he had done the same thing before. He looked at his buddy, who did not seem any wiser to the near accident but was open to conversation. He asked, "Hey, do you want to stop for a quick second? I have to take a leak." As a good friend, he would, and so they did, still trying to listen to the recording that he was sure he played a dozen or so times over, trying to figure out when and where he added the sounds of distant sirens.

At the gas station, they discussed how much longer it would take to complete the trip. His friend joked about how if they were on the freeway, there would be no way that the state patrols would know he did not have a license. Knowing that this was how trips could end in tickets, the entire project of switching drivers was completely squashed. What did matter was if the women that they had somehow managed to attract wouldn't mind hanging out in immediate fashion. It was decided that, yes, they all would make good couples at whichever event they chose to attend. Other than the apparent sense of wrongness, he felt that things could have a bright side.

He did not remember when he began running, only that he had been running for a long enough time that his side began to pinch. Whoever it was that had decided to follow them apparently had a lack of patience because it was not long before it slammed wildly into the car, waving a gun. Only to drive us off the road and pull out a knife that he quickly and deftly jammed into my buddy's neck. Thinking back, he never really saw him hit the ground, but maybe, just maybe, he may be okay. I began to doubt this the longer I ran. The murderer, he calls them now, whoever they were, was persistent because my internal clocks would say it has been maybe a few hours since whoever this maniac was had begun chasing them.

He felt that he was probably the last to live only because of the shrill screams of his female companions. At least, he assumed it was them. He also assumed that whoever this was had only slowed down to take care of them. Funny, he could hear the recordings now repeating the same odd statement. In a desperate plea, he decided to leave another recording, not that it would matter. Listening again, he did not hear his pursuer get close, listening again to the additional sounds of what seemed like a crash. He could feel the knife slam into him a few dozen times before he gurgled himself into unconsciousness.

Shocked again at the surreality of the dream as he has awakened on the toilet of the gas station's restroom. Worried about how terrible the dream or vision actually was, he could not quite remember how he got there. The pain from the dream and the worry of how pieced together his trip was becoming. In all honesty, the last thing he remembered was a terrible accident. And watching his buddy, who now giggled in this attractive woman's face, bleed to death. As her friend sidled up next to him, he jumped and almost knocked the case of beer from her newly inebriated hands. Noticing his buddy's worried expression, he asked him if he was okay, and before he could answer him, he uncharacteristically threatened some odd-looking crossed-eyed guy. The almost confrontation led them to decide to head to a nearby restaurant. One was within walking distance; as they headed to the restaurant, he began to explain about déjà vu. Explaining how the phenomenon was odd and unexplainable, he also tried to explain how he was considering a field in acting. Even though his buddy already had understood this and would remain in support, he explained because it was more for their companions. They decided to play a game to see who would pay for the meal, a game that he lost, so decided to put a limit on the food they would purchase. Reaching into his wallet, he first handed his buddy the recording device. A device he did not have time to try and explain what it was for. Fumbling in his pocket and stepping into the street without looking...

They knew the ambulance would not save him—the force with which he was hit by the truck that looked familiar to some. His buddy bravely called for assistance first, using the recording device in fear or shock. Pressing the record button as if it were a phone and whimpering into the phone, only to glance in shock at his own mistake. Then showing the worried face to the females who, in blank faces, calmly talked to the cops who must've witnessed the horrific ordeal.

"Shivering" or convulsing, either would be the end until he is snatched awake again on the road. Females in tow, not remembering where he picked them up. He and his buddy were now a foursome; it must've been his turn to talk because the car had gone quiet. His friend's determined face was steely on the road. They even passed by the familiar look of some crossed-eyed man who described driving as an adventure and doesn't do it often. They had to depart before they had a chance to explain where they were headed. He fumbled in his pocket for his recording device, a device he did not remember giving to his buddy but only faintly. A device that had not been in his possession for too long, but then again, neither had the photographs that had been in his phone. Pictures of him and his buddy, yeah, but the ones with him and his female companions. Here he is looking at pictures he has no clue to have taken, smiling. Only his smile was odd, almost like it was fake.

The picture did not bother them, only added to the odd amusement. Seemed as if the joke was missing its point when he paid attention to the laughter. Hiding the annoyance he felt when asked about the picture, he jokingly snatched it back from one of the female passengers. He looked at the photo again, not letting the fear cross his face when he noticed that it had changed. Almost as if one of the persons had become aware that someone was looking at them through the photograph. His own face was one of fear and scared him more because he could not make out why he looked that way in the picture that was taken in an unfamiliar setting.

He asked how long they had been driving, and during their brief joyous lecture about time, his friend had to wrench the wheel from the road due to a deer crossing the road. As the car toppled over and over again as if from seemingly no loss of momentum, the passengers who were not in seat belts had the pleasure of being forcefully rattled and thrashed around in the car. He even felt the impact of one of the females' skulls crashing against his own.

He did not remember what came next, based on lying helpless on the ground. Bleeding badly from wounds, it was too dark to see; he could hear growls. The screams from the conscious passengers did not matter as much as the sounds coming from those who had been unconscious. As shadowy shapes descended upon the vehicle, he had the luck to not be in. He slowly lost consciousness as the shapes fell upon him.

Nothing could have happened without the first trip. And the second trip would only be the beginning of another bad story, but what if that could be different? What if…

Nothing could have happened without the second trip. The first trip would only be the beginning of another bad story, but what if that could be different?

He could hear laughter as she let her teeth caress his neck, making a "fart" sound against his neck. He could remember the feeling of possibly her skull colliding against his, as he lazily brushed his hair to the side. After a few brief itinerary discussions, they were ready to descend upon the park. No longer asleep and not sure about what was to come next, he suggested that instead of whatever else we were doing, let's head to the amusement park and get hotel rooms nearby.

It became shockingly clear that this was supposed to happen: the recordings he made and photos that held pictures of people that he barely knew now after a dozen or so trips. He decided to spend this day in an amusement park. I mean, if he was going to die over and over again, which was clear, it might as well happen somewhere fun. Scary, because when he mentioned it to them, it was like he hadn't even said anything. Once, one of them even turned and smiled. Not sure what they heard.

He let the photograph fly from his hand with a brief message on the back and set the recording on the ground…

Vampire Book 1: The Beginning

If the legends were true, then being immortal may be a curse. Depending on how you came to receive this "gift," my story begins here.

Understanding very little about the opportunities of immigrants and even less about the tropics makes the feeling of want and depression that much greater. Having little insight into what makes money or how to attract the right offers for my services. A dealer I am not, or better yet, I am not the dealer of anything that you may not already have. So, my attraction to you and yours to me may seem like a mutual agreement. Like anything that may benefit all parties.

"The warm weather hides the frustration that has creased the brows of the people that pass one another in the streets. The moisture from the passing clouds does not lift the anger from the air."

She notices the angry-looking person with a quizzical expression that hid the apathetic features of her face. The sensual shape is hidden behind long and drab linens that protect her from the heat. To onlookers, she is only a passerby. With the Spanish accents, you can hear people barter for the connection to one another. With the heat and the confusion of tourists, dismay is felt by the natives and those enjoying the sights.

His accent is not quite American but more a mixture of Arabic and Latin and, at times, something else. Catching the phrases at a distance, he can begin to become excited about the coming night and the festival to begin. A heavy drinker and smooth talker, he sees this as a chance to best himself in a "somewhat" foreign place.

She can see the discomfort in the movements of this "man" that she has watched. He seems aware yet nonsensically confident, a trade-off from being in a place that she knows is unfamiliar to him. Following him with light steps and amusement.

Playing cards or shooting pool, deep down, he realizes that he is not the best poker player. He can also almost remember that he probably should not play this far from home, with him being more ill-tempered than noticeable. With high tempers flaring and not being in a "somewhat" familiar place, he decides to find a place to drink and play pool.

He looks out of connection but seems to blend in somehow. She wonders if "he" may be one of "them"—no, the thought quickly fades. Worry sparks the air and soon turns into confidence and then lust. His unawareness and odd demeanor piqued her interest. He is not too tall but taller than some, gangling or something similar. She hmphs, knowing that at this distance he cannot hear her. For this, it is a sure bet that she can see him, and this will not be the last time.

He is still unaware as he flashes a look in her direction. She has already faded into the shadows. He is headed to the closest liquor store, and she is close behind.

Chapter 2

The creeping sensation of annoyance will one day become some diagnosed pain, he thought, and standing in the shade did little to change the mood or temperature. The feeling of Déjà vu on top of Déjà vu settled his nerves into a frenzy. Not bothered by the wait but more by the fact that sleep was short and the mistake of trying to go back to sleep after waking up made him feel a "type" of burn. As the line dwindled down, he accepted his currency in the form of a check, which he knew he could then cash or deposit at a nearby bank.

Her cowled features settled on his brow. She again watched from the shadows with a near sense of memory of the first time she noticed him. Long gone were the feelings of longing, but what did remain was a strong feeling of "something" and a sense of arousal mixed in with hate. In the shadows, the soon-coming dusk played across a smooth and awkwardly plain face. She watched as he distanced himself in long strides. She could feel his thoughts of "bank" and currency and followed.

When he settled down in the chair, he intended to spend as much as he could to feel drunk enough to sleep. He watched the news again as the market coverage spoke about the soon-to-come "Internet," and the effect it would have on the mainstream market. His interested eyes settled on the shape he noticed before, as he looked from the monitor to her, to her, then the monitor. Shocked when she spoke, "Hello."

The conversation was surprisingly interesting, but not because of the words, but more the sense of "her." She had a strong presence but seemed distant. He did not fuss when she seemed to be flirting with someone who happened to jump into the conversation.

Her face masked the way she felt. She said things that seemed like they matched. She had followed and not spoken to him for maybe a week that she barely remembered. She looked at him and did not see a person. She whispered and became excited at his attention. She spoke but did not care about what. She looked and did not feel wrong when she whispered and attracted someone to "their" conversation. The person she had begun to see didn't care for the fact that someone else was there. He tried to fumble with her blouse. "He" cared even less as she touched his hands. Before either could interject, she looked.

He giggled wildly for five minutes as she walked off with another man. He could not see where the conversation went wrong. He felt strange and almost embarrassed about his large outburst of laughter, which only made him laugh more about what happened. He did not miss the newcomer or her for the moment. The suddenness of their departure only made him laugh harder.

The articles will read about this mysterious death. It looked as if the unidentified body may have been torn apart by maybe a pack of wild animals or just one large one. The way it was described says that not much was left of his face, and the cruel twisting of his body said that he possibly could have been torn or pulled apart by something or run over by a car. They could have given details about the attack, but there was not enough blood on the scene to confirm it. People would understand how these things could be confused.

Chapter 3

As she watches the unknown man from the bar, her look of confusion slips into a frown, or rather a cowl of hatred. The unsuspecting victim is not quite drunk but concerned because he does not remember leaving the bar. His slow movements and poor attempt at tracing back his steps only aid his pursuer.

As she tails him, she remembers that she paid at the bar. She did not "whisper or suggest that her drink was free." She left little trace other than what should be a normal occurrence in a place like that. (An attractive woman alone at the bar.) She sees that she may have missed the opportunity for a free drink. Her life has moved well beyond the point of pleasantries.

He is not afraid of the warm air and does not mind the short walk to his hotel. The ending of the conversation, albeit abrupt, does not anger him. Now that he is in the heat, he feels that it may have been better to part.

He feels that the idea of investing money may have been boring to anyone who did not know the language. R.O.I., a simple acronym that could mean a lot. He laughs because that is around where the conversation ended. As he sits down to light a cigarette, he sees he forgot his lighter.

"He mindlessly chuckles as he thinks back to the straight guy named "David." He does not care about sports but does talk about them. "David" mentions that he is somewhat of an athlete and that he smokes. The conversation was interesting because of the mixture. "David" mentions a deal or some bet. "David" also mentioned procurement. As fangs bite deep into his neck and he is violently snatched into an alley, his muffled cry and some sickening sound cannot be heard by passersby.

I Got an Itch: Party Harder!

Jim: From his viewpoint, a party was a party, and that party would not be a party until it was as many people as would fit into the tiny apartment.

With his somewhat inebriated mind, he knew that only a few people would be ready to drive him home. Not being sure of who would be there at night's end and even less sure of who would be ready to drive him home was the last thing on his mind.

From where he stood, this might as well have been as good as any to crash for the night, so he felt the safest thing he could do was drink—not wanting to not fit in.

The cool night air felt a bit dry to him, and he lazily wiped the sweat from his brow…

Bob: Giving Jim a worried glance, he had to stifle a laugh. Not too many times had he known this person to not enjoy a drink. He only worried because of the swaying his friend was doing early into his binge. Noticing that his friend had stepped outside, he wondered if Jim had done so to vomit. Preparing to get a head count of the victims below, he could see that he had not begun to "url" but wipe sweat from his face. As he began to approach him, he heard him muttering something about brains…

Marooney: The party was as successful as he would have hoped it to be. A fair balance, not enough guys that it was a sausage fest and not too many women that they may not decide to let them stag it for the night.

He watched one of them blankly facing a screen, trying to

hear the conversation. He pretended not to notice her and turned his attention toward the screen. "A car that looked like an emergency vehicle had been burned with people around it." Without the volume down, he could not tell the cause. Maybe for the best, not as if his city was doing much better. With local riots and incidents of biting, he felt that worrying right now would not let him enjoy the fun…

Jim: Having recovered from his bout of fatigue, he watched his friend saunter over to him. Trying to avoid the all-to-cliché of clinking bottles, he instead embraced his friend. Laughing, he asked, "What is wrong?"

Bob: Shocked, he only felt relief and answered that he thought "Jim" was sick.

Jim: He said, "Naw, I ain't got it, but some of them might." He turned and pointed to the empty faces they both barely knew. He was saying that he heard someone mentioning something about brains being "juicy." Their exact words may have been, "They brains be juicy as f@#$." Both of them chuckled at the humorous comment. Jim began to explain the rumors he had heard.

Time is inevitable in its pursuit. Things that had felt the cold grasp of death knew that time was no longer an object and that the slowness of death was eternal, creeping in and out of existence. But this hunger was different. It knew neither death nor time; it followed its prey with persistence. This hunger, this itch…

The Story: No one really understood how the fires had started. Feeling at first giddy with safety and warmth, everyone saw the ratio of men to women "comfortable" with an anything goes attitude while they watched fires from the balcony.

The fires at first only seemed to be distant as they would

wander in and out of the small apartment.

Not knowing who came up with the idea to not go outside as a small fight broke out. No one really panicked when it looked as if someone would rush into the party.

All of them at first jokingly said, "You weren't invited." It was funny when they decided to break the rule and "try and let someone in." It shocked no one to see they brought "others." They would all thank whoever decided to barricade the doors. At first, it did not seem like too much.

Time would pass.

They would soon forget how much fun it was, probably when they began to go mad from the persistent "scratching." A scratching that was too soft to be a man and too persistent to be normal. They would soon learn to fear the "sound." It grew quiet...

The partiers knew the risk, and after days of trying to figure out what went wrong that first night, they even talked truthfully about how stupid it was that help could not come. The sad part was they were right.

"All they would have to do was come there and figure out why they wanted to come in."

"Scratch."

Maybe even tell them what made one of them bite someone.

The news copter did not land as they described a gruesome scene. It looked as near as anyone could tell that the party had been raided possibly... It was unclear from this point, and the story went along the lines of gruesome beatings or eatings and bodies that had been too badly mangled to have climbed atop the high rise. Something more about the hunger of "brains."

The police would not let anyone enter, and it had been days since anyone heard from the people inside. No one could understand why they would let "them" in. One cop said, "*Hmph,* I guess he got an itch. Now that you mention it, brains do sound good tonight…"